THE FUNNY THING

BY WANDA GA'G

University of Minnesota Press
Minneapolis • London

The Fesler-Lampert Minnesota Heritage Book Series

This series is published with the generous assistance of the John K. and Elsie Lampert Fesler Fund and David R. and Elizabeth P. Fesler. Its mission is to republish significant out-of-print books that contribute to Minnesota's cultural legacy and to our understanding and appreciation of the Upper Midwest.

ISBN 0-8166-4241-9

A Cataloging-in-Publication record for this book is available from the Library of Congress.

Published by the University of Minnesota Press
111 Third Avenue South, Suite 290
Minneapolis, MN 55401-2520
http://www.upress.umn.edu

Printed in the United States of America on acid-free paper

The University of Minnesota is an equal-opportunity educator and employer.
12 11 10 09 08 07 06 05 04 03   10 9 8 7 6 5 4 3 2 1

THE FUNNY THING

It was a beautiful day in the mountains. The sun was playing hide-and-seek among the fluffy, floating clouds, and the air was soft and warm.

Bobo, the good little man of the mountains, was waiting for the birds and animals to come. To come for what do you suppose? To come for food— because at the door of his mountain cave, Bobo had many good things for them to eat.

He had nut cakes for the
fuzzy tailed squirrels.

He had seed puddings for
the pretty fluttering birds.

He had cabbage salads
for the long-eared rabbits.

He had tiny cheeses—no
bigger than cherries—and
these were for the little mice.

Now on this beautiful sunny day, there came a Funny Thing which Bobo had never seen before. It looked something like a dog and also a little like a giraffe, and from the top of its head to the tip of its curled tail, there was a row of beautiful blue points.

"Good morning," said Bobo. "And what kind of an animal are you?"

"I'm not an animal," said the Funny Thing. "I'm an *aminal!*"

Bobo was about to say that there was no such word as *aminal*, when the Funny Thing looked around fiercely and cried, "And what have you for a hungry *aminal* to eat?"

"Oh," said Bobo, "here are some lovely nut cakes."

"I also have some fine seed puddings."

"This cabbage salad is very nice—"

"—and I'm sure you'd like these little cheeses."

But the Funny Thing turned away and said, "I never heard of such silly food! No *aminal* would eat those things. Haven't you any dolls to-day?"

"Dolls!" cried Bobo in surprise.

"Certainly," said the Funny Thing. "And very good they are—dolls."

"To eat?" cried Bobo, opening his eyes very wide at such an idea.

"To eat, of course," said the Funny Thing smacking his lips. "And very good they are—dolls."

"But it is not kind to eat up little children's dolls," said Bobo, "I should think it would make them very unhappy."

"So it does," said the Funny Thing, smiling pleasantly "but very good they are—dolls."

"And don't the children cry when you take away their dolls?" asked Bobo.

"Don't they though!" said the Funny Thing with a cheerful grin, "but very good they are—dolls."

Tears rolled down Bobo's face as he thought of the Funny Thing going around eating up dear little children's dolls.

"But perhaps you take only naughty children's dolls," he said, brightening up.

"No, I take them specially from good children," said the Funny Thing gleefully, "and *very good* they are — good children's dolls!"

"Oh, what shall I do?" thought Bobo, as he walked back and forth, back and forth. He was trying to think of a plan to make this naughty *aminal* forget to eat dolls.

At last he had an idea!
So he said to the Funny Thing, "What
a lovely tail you have!"

The Funny Thing smiled and wriggled
his tail with a pleased motion.

"And those pretty black eyebrows,"
Bobo continued.

The Funny Thing looked down modestly
and smiled even more.

"But most wonderful of all is that row of blue points down your back," said Bobo.

The Funny Thing was so pleased at this that he rolled foolishly on the ground and smiled very hard.

Then Bobo, who was really a wise old man, said to the Funny Thing, "I suppose you are so beautiful because you eat a great many jum-jills?"

The Funny Thing had never heard of them.

"Jum-jills?" he asked eagerly. "What is a jum-jill—is it a kind of doll?"

"Oh no," said Bobo. "Jum-jills are funny little cakes which make blue points more beautiful, and little tails grow into big ones."

Now the Funny Thing was very vain and there was nothing he would rather have had than a very long tail and bigger and more beautiful blue points. So he cried, "Oh please, dear kind man, give me many jum-jills!"

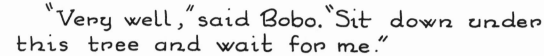

"Very well," said Bobo. "Sit down under this tree and wait for me."

The Funny Thing was all smiles and did as he was told, while Bobo went into his cozy little home, which was like a sort of tunnel under the mountain.

First he had to go through
his little bedroom. Next he came
to his study and finally he reached
the kitchen, where he usually made up
the food for the birds and animals.

Now he took a big bowl, into which he put:
  seven nut cakes
  five seed puddings
  two cabbage salads
  and fifteen little cheeses.
He mixed them with a spoon and rolled
them into little round balls.
  These little balls were jum-jills.

He put them all on a plate and carried them out to the Funny Thing, who was still waiting under the tree.

"Here are your jum-jills," said Bobo, as he handed the plate to the Funny Thing.

The Funny Thing ate one and said,
"And very good they are — jum-jills."

Then he ate another and said,
"And very good they are—jum-jills".

And so on until he had eaten them all up.
"And *very* good they are—jum-jills," he said
with a smack of his lips, after they were all gone.

Then the Funny Thing went home, but the next day he came back for more jum-jills. His tail was already a little longer, his blue points were beginning to grow, and he looked very happy indeed.

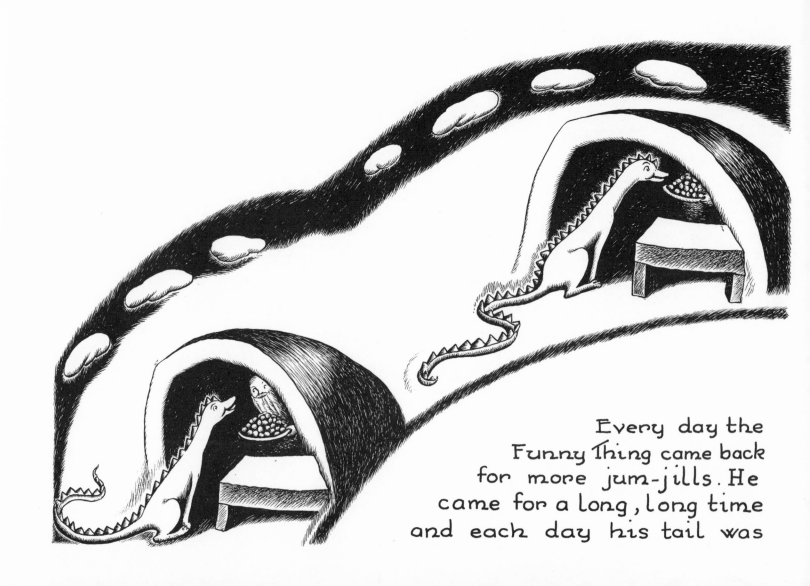

Every day the
Funny Thing came back
for more jum-jills. He
came for a long, long time
and each day his tail was

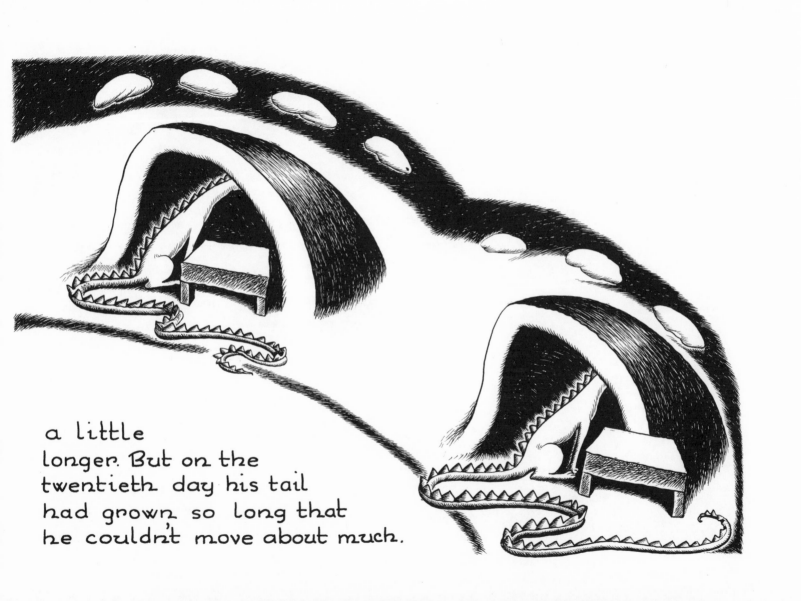

a little
longer. But on the
twentieth day his tail
had grown so long that
he couldn't move about much.

So he chose a
nice big mountain and
sat on the very top of it. Every
day Bobo sent birds to carry jum-jills
to the Funny Thing, and as the Funny Thing's
tail grew longer and longer, he curled it
contentedly around his mountain.

His one joy in life was his beautiful blue-pointed tail, and by and by
the only words he ever said were:
"And very good they are—
jum-jills!"

So of course he ate no
more dolls and we have kind
old Bobo to thank for that.

THE END